Raj

the Bookstore Tiger

Kathleen T. Pelley   Illustrated *by* Paige Keiser

Charlesbridge

For Shashi, Bipin, and Winnie—in memory of your sweet Yamini,
whose spirit still burns bright
—K. T. P.

In loving memory of my best friend, Erika Cadran
—P. K.

First paperback edition 2012
Text copyright © 2011 by Kathleen T. Pelley
Illustrations copyright © 2011 by Paige Keiser

Published by Charlesbridge
85 Main Street
Watertown, MA 02472
(617) 926-0329
www.charlesbridge.com

Library of Congress Cataloging-in-Publication Data
Pelley, Kathleen T.
   Raj the bookstore tiger / Kathleen T. Pelley ; illustrated by Paige Keiser.
     p. cm.
   Summary: When a new manager brings Snowball, a grouchy cat, to the shop where Raj and
his owner live and work, Snowball informs Raj that he is not the tiger everyone believes him to be.
   ISBN 978-1-58089-230-8 (reinforced for library use)
   ISBN 978-1-58089-231-5 (softcover)
[1. Cats—Fiction. 2. Tigers—Fiction. 3. Self-perception—Fiction. 4. Bookstores—Fiction.
5. Human-animal relationships—Fiction.] I. Keiser, Paige, ill. II. Title.
PZ7.P3645Raj 2011
[E]—dc22   2010007585

Printed in China
(hc) 10 9 8 7 6 5 4 3 2 1
(sc) 10 9 8 7 6 5 4 3 2 1

Illustrations done in Winsor & Newton tube watercolors and Prismacolor colored pencil on hot press
   Arches watercolor paper
Display type and text type set in Curlz MT and Berkeley Oldstyle
Color separations by Chroma Graphics, Singapore
Printed and bound February 2012 by Jade Productions in Heyuan, Guangdong, China
Production supervision by Brian G. Walker
Designed by Diane M. Earley

Raj was a tiger. Not a jungle tiger or an Indian tiger, but a tiger all the same. That's what Felicity Fotheringham had called him the day she brought him home to her attic above the bookstore she owned.

"What a tiger!" Felicity had gasped as she held him up to the sun. "Look at that gorgeous golden coat! And those beautiful chocolate stripes! Only a real tiger's name is good enough for you. I will call you Raj."

Being a bookstore tiger was hard work. Mornings began with a patrol of the storerooms, followed by sun basking in the front window. And if a passerby rattled the window, Raj never flinched. He just chimed to himself,

"I'm a tiger! I'm a tiger! I'm a tiger!"

Then, after a face wash and a snooze, it was time to
greet the customers with a leg rub or a hearty meow.

But it was the afternoon story time that Raj loved best.
After Felicity had gathered the children, she would announce,
"Now let's welcome a special guest—Raj, our very own
bookstore tiger." That was Raj's signal to strut forward,
eyes flashing and tail swishing, as he chanted to himself, "I'm a tiger!"

I'm a tiger! I'm a tiger!"

"Look!" the children squealed. "It's a little tiger!"
Then they tickled his chin, scratched his ears, and argued
over whose lap he would share.

Every evening, back at the attic, Raj curled up to sleep at
the foot of Felicity's bed. And so life for Raj was as charmed
as any fairy tale he had ever heard, until . . .

One day the new manager, Christopher Cuthbert, told
Felicity that he was having problems with his cat, Snowball.
"Ever since we got our Labrador puppy, Snowball has
turned mean and cranky," he said. "My poor wife is at her
wits' end."

"Well, why don't you bring Snowball here during the day?" Felicity suggested. "He might be happier, and I'm sure he won't be a bit of bother to anyone."

But as it turned out, Snowball *was* a bother . . . to Raj.

"Who are you?" demanded Snowball the moment
Christopher plunked him down in the window next to Raj.

So startled was Raj that his tail squiggled and his purr
vanished.

"I'm Raj. Raj, the tiger."

Snowball sniggered. "Don't be ridiculous! Tigers are wild beasts that live in the jungle and roar like thunder."

Raj took a step backward. "But . . . but . . . but I *am* a tiger," he spluttered. "Everyone says so. That's why they call me the bookstore tiger."

Snowball snorted. "That's just a joke, son. You're not a real tiger. In fact, you're just a plain old marmalade kitty-cat with muddy brown splotches that some people might call stripes. Now, run along. I need to catch up on my nap, thanks to that yappy new puppy back home."

Raj stalked off, head held as high as he could muster.

He hid in the storeroom,
mulling over Snowball's words.

By closing time Raj was a huddled
hump beneath Felicity's chair.

At bedtime he burrowed beneath
a pillow and fell asleep in a dark hole.

From then on, Raj was either crouched beneath a chair in the attic or huddled in a hump atop one of the bookstore's shelves. "I'm just a plain old kitty-cat," he told himself over and over.

He didn't come down for story time, not even when he saw Snowball sprawled in a child's lap with a smirk spread across his face.

One night as Raj hid beneath Felicity's chair,
he heard her reading aloud from a book. " 'Tyger! Tyger!
burning bright / In the forests of the night,' " she said.
Raj poked his head out and peered at Felicity. "Yes, Raj,"
she whispered. "Isn't this a splendid poem by Mr. Blake?
I knew you'd like it."

Slowly Raj crawled up into Felicity's lap. He sat there purring loudly all evening as she read the poem to him again and again.

In the morning Raj greeted Felicity with his best tiger roar, followed by a pretend ambush and some dust-mote swatting.

"Why, Raj, my little tiger," cooed Felicity, "I believe
you're back to your old self. Wait till you see what I've
got planned for you today!"

Off they went to open the bookstore.

By the time Snowball arrived, Raj was basking in the window.

"Move over, sonny," ordered Snowball. "No room for joke tigers here."

But Snowball's jibes had lost their sting. Raj didn't budge—not even when Snowball hissed and scowled.

At story time Raj watched from a high shelf as
Snowball sprawled across two children's laps. Felicity
clapped her hands and announced, "Today we have a
special guest—author Sanjiv Patel. He's going to show us
a video about India, where all his stories take place."

Raj peered closer now. The lights dimmed. Pictures appeared on the screen. The sound of rain gushed from the speakers. "This is the jungle during our rainy season—the monsoon," Sanjiv said. "And this is our very own Bengal tiger." A roar ripped through the store.

Suddenly Snowball fluffed up his fur, hissed at the screen, and fled in a streak of white.

Raj, too, felt a stab of fear. But then he remembered his poem. The words made him feel bold and brave and . . . tigerish.

Raj sprang to the floor and reared up in front of the screen, eyes flashing and tail lashing.

"Why, look!" cried Sanjiv. "It's a little tiger!"

"Yes," said Felicity, "this is our other special guest, Raj—our bookstore tiger." Raj strutted around the children as they squealed and giggled and pointed.

Later, when Sanjiv and the children had
left, Snowball sidled up to Raj and whined,
"No matter what they say, you're still just—"

OPEN!

Story Time
THURSDAYS 1:00-1:30

TAJ
MAHAL

TODAY
Author
Sanjiv
Patel
1:30-2:00

"Did you know," Raj interrupted him, "that there's a picture of a tiger in that book over there? And it's white— just like you."

Snowball sniffed. "Hmm . . . a white tiger, you say?"

Snowball gazed at the picture for a long time.
He blinked. Finally he purred.

"Come on," said Raj, nudging Snowball. "Let's make
the rounds together."

"Okay . . . tiger," agreed Snowball.

Eyes flashing, tails swishing, off they went, chanting,

"I'm a tiger! I'm a tiger! I'm a tiger!"